Captain Hawk and the Stone of Destiny

Jim Eldridge

Illustrated by Janek Matysiak

A & C Black · London

Chapter One

Captain James Hawk put his tiny, battered spacecraft into a dive, barely escaping the laser burst from the AnPod starfighter. Then he hurtled back up again as two more starfighters headed straight for him.

7

Hawk pulled back on the steering control. He sent his spacecraft spinning, as if out of control, straight into the path of one of the oncoming starfighters.

In a panic the pilot of the starfighter changed course. But he found himself heading straight into another starfighter which was coming at Hawk from the other direction.

Xan-X looked at the approaching
starfighters and made what in human
sounds would have been a gulp.

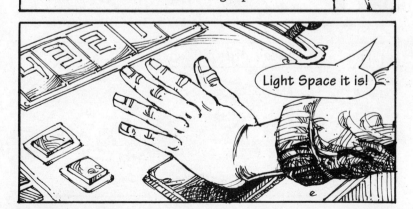

11

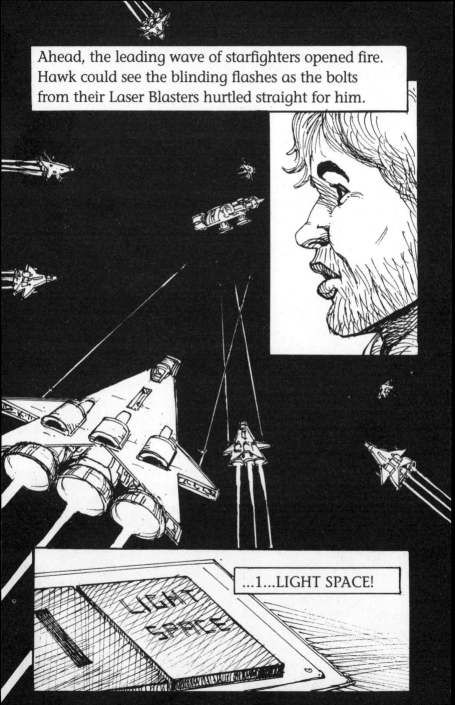

Ahead, the leading wave of starfighters opened fire. Hawk could see the blinding flashes as the bolts from their Laser Blasters hurtled straight for him.

...1...LIGHT SPACE!

13

The next second Hawk and Xan-X were in a tunnel of lights and the starfighters and laser fire were fast disappearing behind them.

Yes!!! We're safe! We've done it! We're...

He stopped and stared as they left Light Space.

Who put that planet there?!

Ahead of them, increasing in size with every milli-second, was a huge planet zooming towards them.

I did warn you, sir. It would appear that we have materialised inside the gravitational pull of a Class M planet, which...

Stop yacking and get your head down! We're gonna crash!

Then they were plunging towards the mass ahead...

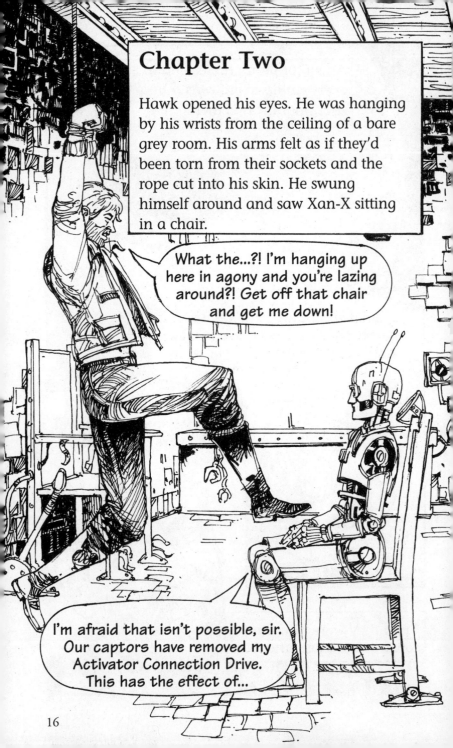

Chapter Two

Hawk opened his eyes. He was hanging by his wrists from the ceiling of a bare grey room. His arms felt as if they'd been torn from their sockets and the rope cut into his skin. He swung himself around and saw Xan-X sitting in a chair.

What the...?! I'm hanging up here in agony and you're lazing around?! Get off that chair and get me down!

I'm afraid that isn't possible, sir. Our captors have removed my Activator Connection Drive. This has the effect of...

'Forget it,' said Hawk. 'Right at this moment I don't need to know your medical problems. Where are we?'

Hawk thought it over for a moment.

'Okay,' he said. 'Number one good point: my mouth is uninjured, so with a bit of luck I should be able to talk us out of this.' He grinned confidently. 'There is no one in the Universe able to withstand the quick brain and even quicker tongue of Captain James Hawk!'

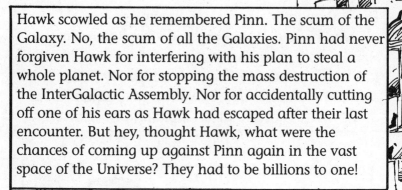

Hawk scowled as he remembered Pinn. The scum of the Galaxy. No, the scum of all the Galaxies. Pinn had never forgiven Hawk for interfering with his plan to steal a whole planet. Nor for stopping the mass destruction of the InterGalactic Assembly. Nor for accidentally cutting off one of his ears as Hawk had escaped after their last encounter. But hey, thought Hawk, what were the chances of coming up against Pinn again in the vast space of the Universe? They had to be billions to one!

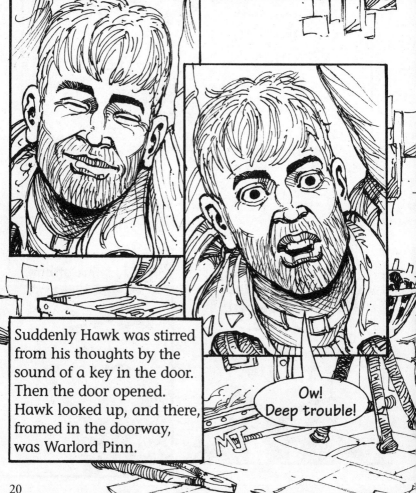

Suddenly Hawk was stirred from his thoughts by the sound of a key in the door. Then the door opened. Hawk looked up, and there, framed in the doorway, was Warlord Pinn.

Ow!
Deep trouble!

And Pinn talked, mainly about something called the Stone of Destiny, and Hawk listened. By the time Pinn had finished Hawk looked even more uncomfortable than he had before.

'Let me run this through again, just to make sure I've got it right,' said Hawk. 'You want me to go back to AnPod Space, from where I've just barely escaped with my life, and steal a small piece of rock from a Shape Shifter called GGan. Shape Shifters, as we know, can change themselves to look like anything at all: people, rocks, liquids, so they're not particularly easy to spot. Also, this particular Shape Shifter, GGan, has this Stone of Destiny hidden in some secret place where it's guarded by some slime horror with razor sharp teeth called a Nnn.'

How am I doing so far?

Very good. Your powers of recall have improved since we last met.

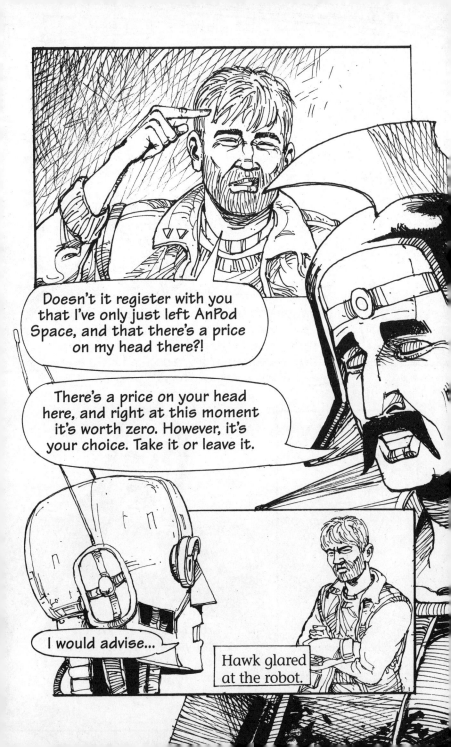

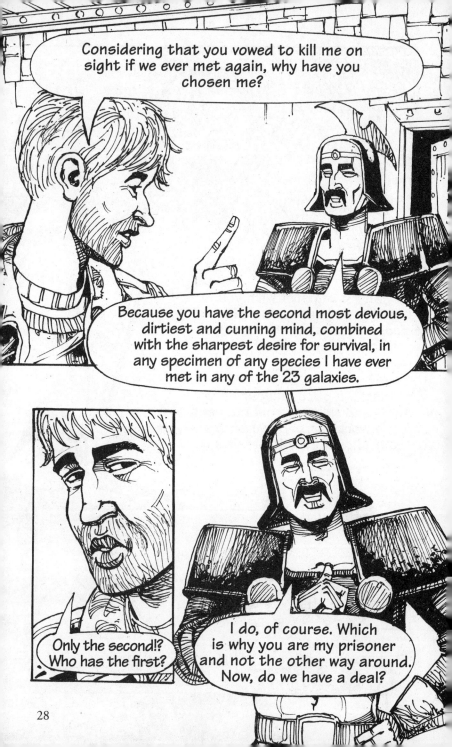

28

'Okay, it's a deal,' said Hawk. 'If you just put us back on our ship, we'll be on our way.'

'Not so fast,' said Pinn, and he smiled. It was one of the worst sights that Xan-X had ever seen.

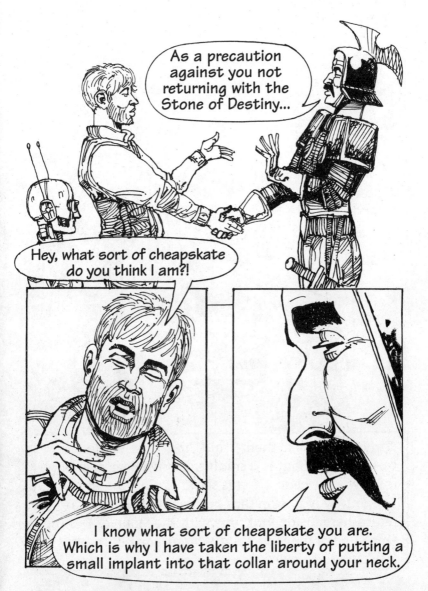

Collar?

Hawk felt around his neck. It was the first time he'd noticed he'd even got it on, the metal was so light. Then he noticed that Xan-X had an identical collar around his neck too.

Hey! A fashion statement. Groovy!

'I'm glad you like them,' said Pinn. 'The implant I was talking about is a small explosive device, enough to blow your head off. It is set to explode in 48 hours. The only way to stop that happening is for you to return here inside that time with the Stone of Destiny. Once I have the Stone in my hand, I will turn off the explosive devices.'

Chapter Four

Back at the controls of his spacecraft, Hawk was about to enter Light Space again on their return to AnPod.

Of course, he could be lying about these collars being booby-trapped.

I don't think so, sir. The Warlord Pinn struck me as most truthful on that part of his statement.

I suppose there's only one way to find out.

You're not thinking of trying to take off your collar?
No, I was going to suggest you try.
But...!!
After all, you are a robot. I can rebuild you.

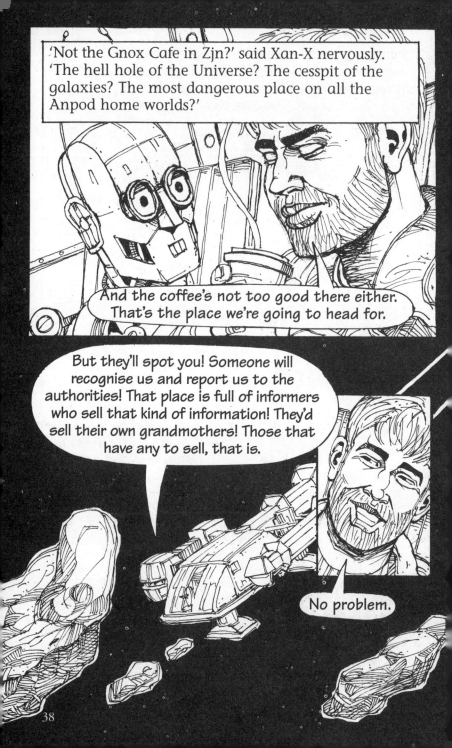

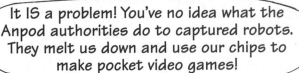

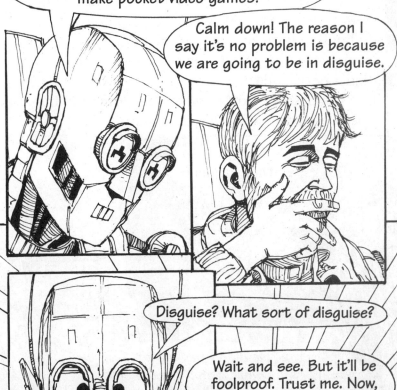

Hawk slammed his hand down on the Light Space Activator, and once more they sped into the tunnel of lights.

39

Chapter Five

The Gnox Cafe in Zjn, the capital of the AnPod home worlds, was one of the seediest places in the whole galaxy. Here everything could be bought, from androids to assassinations, with wholescale rebellions available at a high price, and information at an even higher price. Sudden death, however, was cheap, as Hawk and Xan-X noticed when they arrived at the cafe: a body was just being thrown out.

Xan-X looked about him nervously as they went in. The journey to Zjn had been nerve-wracking enough once they had left Light Space. Hawk had had to fly in the radio shadow of an AnPod freighter to fool any watching and waiting Military Craft. But now, disguised as a pair of wandering entertainers, Xan-X felt they fooled no one.

For one thing they looked ridiculous. And what if they should be called on to entertain someone? Like the owner of this cafe, for example? Would they end up in the gutter, like the poor wretch they had just seen?

43

That's my business.

...is your business. My business is the fact that I know where there might be one, and fortunately for you, it's right here on this planet.

'Wow!!' pretended Hawk. 'Now that's what I call a coincidence!'

'Hardly, sir,' corrected Xan-X. 'If you remember... Ow!!'

This 'Ow!!' followed a sharp clonk as Hawk kicked Xan-X under the table, jarring the electrodes in the robot's knee joint.

Tell me about the Nnn.

This place has *too* many ears. Meet me outside in fifteen minutes.

With that, the rat-like Jassa slipped away through the crowded cafe.

But as they rose to their feet, they felt strong paws on their shoulders pushing them back down. Looking up, they found themselves gazing into the hideous faces of a pair of giant Slumgums, half slug, half ape, each well over three metres tall and a metre wide.

47

The two Slumgums exchanged puzzled frowns.

'I'm not giving presents this year,' said Hawk.
'Only donations to my favourite charity, which is
me. So if you'll just take your great paws off...'
  A growling noise came from the second Slumgum.
'What you do if we don't?!' snarled the Slumgum
nastily. 'You beat us over head with song?'

The Slumgum released its grip on Hawk. The next second there was a deafening BLAMMBLAMM!! as Hawk pulled out his Laser Blaster and hit both Slumgums with a burst which dropped them to the floor, unconscious.

I said I'd let them have it. I didn't say what.

'It was lucky you had your Laser Blaster on 'stun' and not 'kill', or you could have committed a serious offence,' said Xan-X, as they pushed their way out of the cafe.

The next second the ground around them rose up, and a rush of air lifted them off their feet, spinning them round and round.

'It's a tornado!' yelled Hawk, desperately trying to remember which way was up as the tornado hurled them round and round inside its spinning vortex.

Chapter Six

Minutes later, Hawk and Xan-X found themselves shackled to giant bolts sunk into the rock wall of a deep cave.

If you're about to say that sounds like a slithering and slurping sound, forget it! I can hear it for myself. I suggest you hurry up and examine options four thousand and four and beyond, before we end up in deep trouble!

As they listened the slithering and slurping sound drew nearer. Suddenly there was a low roar immediately behind them, then a burst of foul-smelling air rolled over Hawk and Xan-X.

Wow! Bad breath!!

They turned to find themselves face to face with a huge red mass. In the centre of what could be called its face was a tiny glowing eye. Below this eye was a set of huge pointed teeth. Hawk watched in horror as the teeth began to separate and the Nnn's hideous mouth began to open.

I think it's lunchtime! And I don't mean ours!

I think, sir, I now have an idea how to get out of this!

This is no time to discuss it! Just do it!

With supersonic speed, Xan-X unclipped his arms and legs from his body and slipped out of the shackles and chains. Then he reclipped his limbs back into position.

If you're about to suggest I do that...

Wait..!

Suddenly, before Hawk could shout at him to stop, Xan-X jumped straight into the Nnn's now gaping mouth. Hawk gasped, stunned.

No!! My only friend..!!

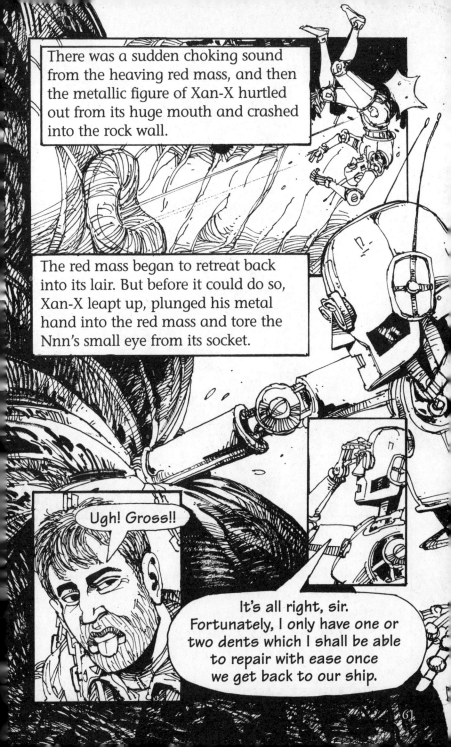

But pulling out the Nnn's eye like that..!

'Exactly!' said Xan-X triumphantly. 'My plan was based on my sensors informing me that the Nnn was blind. Therefore it couldn't see us, only sense us. Once it realised that the first one of us it tried to eat was made of metal and therefore of low taste quality, my theory was that it would think the same was true of both of us, and give up trying to eat us.'

Chapter Seven

Hawk sat at the controls of his spacecraft, once again flying in the radio shadow of a freighter fleet to fool any waiting AnPod military craft.

'Of course,' he said, 'I guessed that the Nnn's eye was the Stone of Destiny all the time. I was just waiting for my chance to grab it.'

Of course, sir. Actually, I hope it won't embarrass you if I express my gratitude for the concern you showed back in the cave, when I leapt into the Nnn's mouth and you described me as your only friend...

Hawk wriggled uncomfortably in his seat.

Listen. I didn't mean that you're my ONLY friend. I've got friends all over the galaxies. I mean, there's...there's...

Yes, sir?

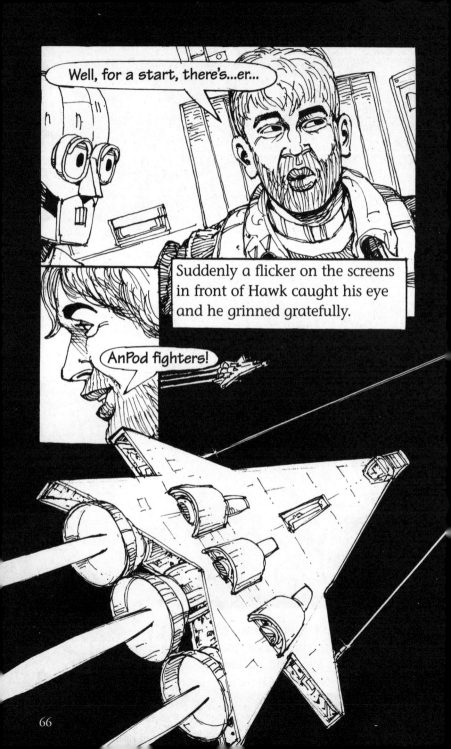

The next second a hail of laser fire began to open up, scorching into the hull of their spacecraft and sending them reeling wildly.

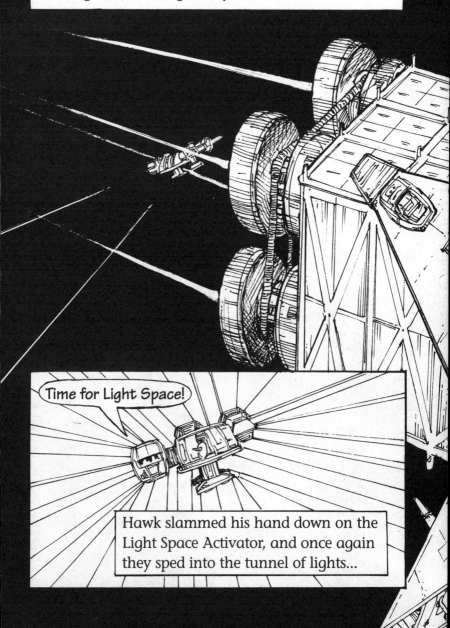

Chapter Eight

Hawk and Xan-X watched as Pinn inspected the small stone in his hand. Surrounding them were six of Pinn's Inner Guards, all of whom pointed laser weapons at their heads.

'You lied about the collars having explosive devices?' asked Hawk.

'No, I lied about our deal,' said Pinn. 'Now I've got the Stone I shall blow your heads off.' He picked up the remote control, his thumb poised over the explosive button.

'I guessed you might pull a stunt like this, so I put the real stone somewhere very very safe,' said Hawk. 'If you don't believe me, try asking that piece of rock in your hand something about the future, and see if it gives you an answer.'

Pinn went deathly white, then purple with anger. He looked down at the stone in his hand.

What will happen to Captain Hawk?

The stone stayed mute, glowing quietly, saying nothing.

See?

Pinn let out a roar of rage and leapt at Hawk, grabbing him round the neck.

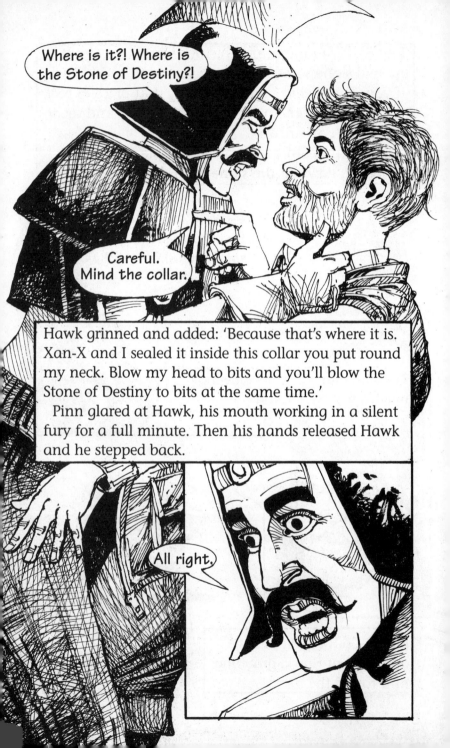

Hawk grinned and added: 'Because that's where it is. Xan-X and I sealed it inside this collar you put round my neck. Blow my head to bits and you'll blow the Stone of Destiny to bits at the same time.'

Pinn glared at Hawk, his mouth working in a silent fury for a full minute. Then his hands released Hawk and he stepped back.

He pressed a switch on the Remote Activator and there was a click from the collars around their necks.

Then, before anyone apart from Xan-X realised what was happening, Hawk pulled a blind grenade from his pocket. He threw it at Pinn, and turned away, his eyes shut tight.

The white light from the silently exploding grenade filled the room, blinding Pinn and his Inner Guards. While Pinn and his men were helpless Xan-X and Hawk worked swiftly.

By the time they could see again, Xan-X had fixed both collars around Pinn's neck and Hawk was just finishing keying in the re-activator on the Remote Control.

There! You wanted the Stone of Destiny, Pinn, now you've got it.

Hawk and Xan-X rushed out of the room, pulling the door shut behind them and slipping the bolt. From the other side of the door they could hear hammering and shouting as Pinn and the Inner Guards began to panic.

Fifty nine minutes, Pinn! Ask the Stone what your destiny is!